DATE DUE

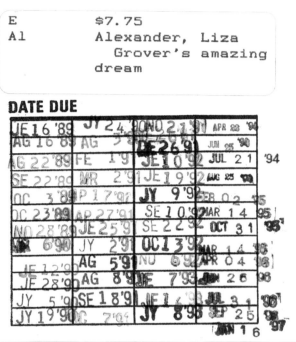

Grover's Amazing Dream

A Storybook Introducing New Words

By Liza Alexander / Illustrated by Tom Cooke

Featuring Jim Henson's Sesame Street Muppets

A Sesame Street/Golden Press Book
Published by Western Publishing Company, Inc.,
in conjunction with Children's Television Workshop.

Note to Parents

Language is a central part of a child's world. As preschoolers, children acquire basic words from parents' conversation and extend their vocabularies through exposure to television, books, and magazines. *Grover's Amazing Dream* intentionally uses unusual and sophisticated words to help expand your child's vocabulary. Some of the words Grover uses to describe his dream might be new to your child, but he or she should be able to grasp the meanings of the unfamiliar words in the context of the story and its pictures. If your child has difficulty understanding a particular word, make up new sentences together that are meaningful to your child and that use the word correctly.

A growing vocabulary helps your child communicate effectively and will later be crucial to a variety of school activities. In this story Grover's descriptive language is often evocative of sight, sound, smell, or touch. The sounds of some of these words are intriguing to children. These words are also fun to say. Learning about words and their meaning can be a challenging and satisfying experience for children and the beginning of a good lifelong habit.

Grover snoozed happily in his bed. His head rested softly on his fluffy pillow. His furry blue body was warm under his fuzzy blue blanket.

Even though Grover was asleep, he knew his mommy was cooking breakfast. He heard the pop of the toaster and the sizzle of the bacon on the griddle.

Creak! went the stairs as Mommy climbed up to Grover's room. "It's time for breakfast, dear," said Mommy. "Rise and shine!"

But Grover just sighed and tugged his blanket closer to him. He was still dreaming.

Mommy tiptoed over to Grover and perched on the edge of his bed. Grover rolled over, rubbed his eyes, and stretched.

"Oh, Mommy!" he said. "I just had the most amazing dream!"

"Really, dear?" asked Mommy. "Tell me about it!"

"Well," said Grover, "I was in a canoe on a stream in a jungle. The water lapped against my boat. My oar splish-splashed as I paddled to the shore.

"I leapt out. Water sloshed around my feet.
I dragged my canoe—thump, thump—up the bank.
I parked the canoe beside a gnarled tree!
    "It was very noisy in the jungle.... The bugs buzzed!
The monkeys screeched! Near the ground the bushes
were tangled with ugly weeds and beautiful blossoms.
Tall trees towered above me.

"Then, Mommy, I grabbed a vine and began to swing from vine to vine, tree to tree. I soared as high as the sky! Oh, my goodness, it was scary, but then I swung back down to the ground and everything was all right. I was safe and sound. Phew!"

"Grover, were you looking at that jungle book again last night?" asked Mommy.

"Well, yes," said Grover, "but there is more to my dream!

"Suddenly I saw a swamp. I walked toward it and crushed many brushy ferns and leafy bushes with my big blue feet. I stepped into the swamp, and my feet went squish, squish in the gooey mud.

"'Eeew!' I gasped. A snake slinked across the swamp,
and I watched him slither up a tree.

"The snake hissed, 'S'long!' through his fangs. He
slipped away into the branches. I could not see him
anymore."

Grover paused for a moment in telling his dream.
Mommy smoothed his sheets and plumped his pillow.
"What's this doing here?" she asked as she pulled a
book out from under the covers. "Is this the library
book you checked out yesterday?"

"Yes," said Grover, "but, Mommy, my amazing
dream goes on and on! Then I dreamed that I was on
top of a snow-capped mountain. Brrrrrr!

"My teeth were chattering. I felt goose bumps on my arms and legs. I was shivering!

"Still, I jumped on a swift wooden sled and zoomed down the mountain through the trees. Snowflakes whirled and the wind howled. The trees were heavy with snow and icicles. A branch snapped and its load of snow thudded to the ground. The sled ride never seemed to end!

"Finally my sled slowed down. I slid onto a frozen pond and found some ice skates. I laced them on. On the ice I twirled and jumped. I traced a figure eight. I was very graceful! Amazing!"

"Well, well," said Mommy, picking up something from the floor. "Not another book!" She added it to the pile on Grover's bed.

"Yes," said Grover, "I was reading last night to make me sleepy. Mommy, there is more to my dream. Listen! Next it was springtime. I wandered in the forest. The breeze whispered through the trees. The ground was bright with tiny flowers.

"I rested on a cushion of velvety green moss and listened to the sounds," said Grover.

"The steps of a little squirrel went pitter-patter. Plunk! He dropped some nuts into a hollow tree. Rat-a-tat-tat! A woodpecker hammered his beak into a tree trunk. Tweet, tweet! Birds chirped. The forest was alive with sound!

"Before I knew it, the sounds were hushed and the forest was quiet. I opened my eyes to see that all the trees and flowers were drenched with dew. They glistened in the twilight.

"Night fell. The dark was soothing," said Grover, sighing. "I curled up and was lulled to sleep."

Mommy shook Grover's shoulders gently and went to get his robe. "Don't go back to sleep now, little Grover. It really is time to get up."

Grover opened his eyes and stretched once again. "Was that not an amazing dream?"

"Yes, you certainly have a vivid imagination, dear! Now, up and at 'em!" said Mommy.

Whoops! Mommy stumbled over another book that was on the floor. She stooped down and picked it up and asked Grover, "Don't tell me you read all these books before you went to sleep? *Jungle Days*, *Tales of the Swamp*, *The Snow Bunny*, *Forest Frolics*. You little monster! No wonder you dreamed your amazing dream!"